When God Makes Scribbles Beautiful

Kate Rietema

Illustrated by Jennie Poh

B&H kids

Brentwood TN

To all the children who became part of our family
through foster care.—Kate

For the Edwards family, with love.—Jennie

He has made everything beautiful in its time.
Also, he has put eternity into man's heart,
yet so that he cannot find out what God has
done from the beginning to the end.

—Ecclesiastes 3:11, ESV

Text Copyright © 2023 by Kate Rietema
Illustrations Copyright © 2023 by B&H Publishing Group
Published by B&H Publishing Group, Brentwood, Tennessee
All rights reserved. ISBN: 978-1-0877-8766-4
Author is represented by the literary agency of Credo Communications LLC,
Grand Rapids, Michigan, www.credocommunications.net.
Scripture references are taken from: The Holy Bible, English Standard Version®
Copyright © 2001 by Crossway Bibles, a publishing ministry of Good News Publishers.
Christian Standard Bible®, Copyright © 2017 by Holman Bible Publishers. Used by
permission. Christian Standard Bible® and CSB® are federally registered trademarks of
Holman Bible Publishers. The Holy Bible, International Children's Bible®
Copyright© 1986, 1988, 1999, 2015 by Thomas Nelson. Used by permission.
Dewey Decimal Classification: CE
SH: PROVIDENCE AND GOVERNMENT OF GOD \ SUFFERING \ JOY AND SORROW
Printed in Heshan, Guangdong, China, September 2023
1 2 3 4 5 6 · 27 26 25 24 23

Sometimes, hard things happen.

It might feel like a dark scribble.

And you will probably
feel lonely.

Or sad.

Or angry.

Or scared.

Or maybe everything
all at the same time.

The dark scribble follows you everywhere.

If you hide from it, it finds you.

If you ignore it, it's still there.

If you yell, "Go away!" the scribble doesn't listen.

What can you do?

You can say,

"God, help me!"

And little bit by little bit, He will.

Give all your worries to him, because he cares for you. —1 Peter 5:7, ICB

God will give you what you need—

Sunshine if you feel cold inside,

. . . *God will supply all your needs.* —Philippians 4:19, CSB

a friend if you
want company,

or something funny
if you need to laugh.

11

Even if more scribbles come, don't worry.
God has a good plan.

It might feel hard to believe, but it's true.

And nothing can mess up God's plan—
not even lots and lots of scribbles.

"For I know the plans I have for you...
to give you a future and a hope." —Jeremiah 29:11, CSB

It may feel like His plan takes forever to happen.

You might have to wait.

The Lord is not slow in doing what he promised . . . —2 Peter 3:9, ICB

And wait.

And wait.

Wait for the Lord; be strong, and let your heart be courageous.
Wait for the Lord. —Psalm 27:14, CSB

Waiting is hard.

17

But God will be with you while you wait.

You won't be able to see God with your eyes,
but you will know He's there in a feeling-sort-of-way.

"...God is with you wherever you go." —Joshua 1:9, CSB

Slowly, God takes every hard thing, and He mixes in love and light.

The scribbles are still there,
but God changes them into something new.

He has made everything beautiful in its time. —Ecclesiastes 3:11, ESV

Maybe the scribbles become steppingstones,
leading you somewhere wonderful and surprising.

Maybe the scribbles drift into the distance, like clouds at sunset.

You look at them
and say, "Wow!"

...all things work together for the good
of those who love God ... —Romans 8:28, CSB

And God changes you too.

Maybe you feel strong
enough to climb a
tree so magnificent
you can see for miles;

...troubles produce patience ...
character ... hope. —Romans 5:3–4, ICB

or perhaps you feel quiet enough
to lay in the grass and listen to
the murmur of the meadow;

or you might feel so joyful
that you stand on a stone
and sing as loud as you can.

27

You will have grown on the inside.

And when you notice someone else with a scribble, you will be ready to help.

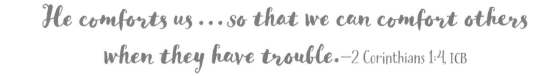

He comforts us . . . so that we can comfort others when they have trouble. —2 Corinthians 1:4, ICB

You are kind to her.

Then one day, you show her your steppingstones
and let her see your clouds at sunset.

You teach her how to say, "God, help me!"

And little bit by little bit…

He will.